DISCOVER SERIES
MUSICAL
INSTRUMENTS

Accordian

Banjo

Bongo Drum

Cello

Clarinet

Concertina

Drums

Electric Guitar

Flute

French Horn

Guitar

Harp

Mandolin

Maracas

Microphone

Piano

Saxaphone

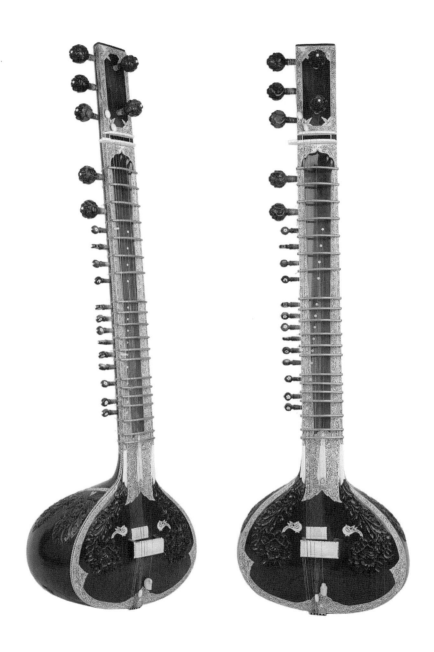

Sitars

Trombone

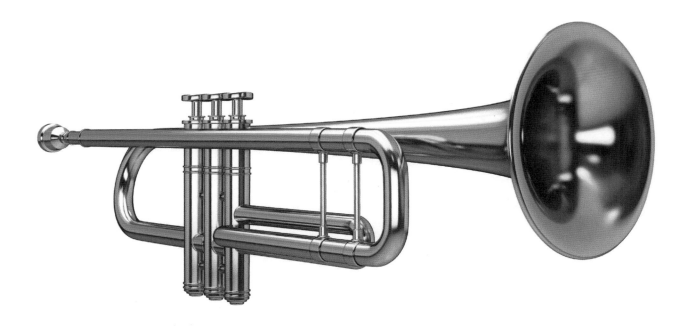

Trumpet

Violin

Make Sure to Check Out the Other Discover Series Books from Xist Publishing:

Published in the United States by Xist Publishing
www.xistpublishing.com
PO Box 61593 Irvine, CA 92602

© 2012 by Xist Publishing
All rights reserved
No portion of this book may be reproduced without express permission of the publisher
All images licensed from Fotolia
First Edition

ISBN-13: 978-1-62395-066-8 • ISBN-10: 162395066X

xist Publishing

Made in the USA
Lexington, KY
04 February 2014